Community Helpers

Park Rangers

by Erika S. Manley

Bullfrog Books

Ideas for Parents and Teachers

Bullfrog Books let children practice reading informational text at the earliest reading levels. Repetition, familiar words, and photo labels support early readers.

Before Reading

- Discuss the cover photo. What does it tell them?
- Look at the picture glossary together. Read and discuss the words.

Read the Book

- "Walk" through the book and look at the photos. Let the child ask questions. Point out the photo labels.
- Read the book to the child, or have him or her read independently.

After Reading

- Prompt the child to think more. Ask: Did you know about park rangers before reading this book? What more would you like to learn about them?

Bullfrog Books are published by Jump!
5357 Penn Avenue South
Minneapolis, MN 55419
www.jumplibrary.com

Copyright © 2020 Jump! International copyright reserved in all countries. No part of this book may be reproduced in any form without written permission from the publisher.

Library of Congress Cataloging-in-Publication Data

Names: Manley, Erika S., author.
Title: Park rangers / by Erika S. Manley.
Description: Bullfrog books edition. Minneapolis, MN: Jump!, Inc., [2020]
Series: Community helpers
Audience: Age 5–8.
Audience: K to Grade 3. Includes index.
Identifiers: LCCN 2018055997 (print)
LCCN 2018057622 (ebook)
ISBN 9781641288330 (ebook)
ISBN 9781641288316 (hardcover : alk. paper)
ISBN 9781641288323 (paperback)
Subjects: LCSH: Park rangers—Juvenile literature.
Classification: LCC SB481.3 (ebook)
LCC SB481.3 .M36 2020 (print) | DDC 363.6/8—dc23
LC record available at https://lccn.loc.gov/2018055997

Editor: Jenna Trnka
Designer: Shoreline Publishing Group

Photo Credits: Jeff Schultz/Alaska Images/SuperStock, cover, 12–13, 23tl; Steve Bly/Alamy, 1; Jamirae/Adobe Stock, 3; National Park Service, 4, 5, 8–9, 10, 14–15, 16–17, 18, 19, 23bl, 23br; M2 Photography/Alamy, 6–7, 23tr; FotoVoyager/iStock, 11; Alaska Stock/SuperStock, 20–21; Natural History Library/Alamy, 22; Natural History Archive/Alamy, 24.

Printed in the United States of America at Corporate Graphics in North Mankato, Minnesota.

Table of Contents

Park Protectors	4
At the Visitor Center	22
Picture Glossary	23
Index	24
To Learn More	24

Park Protectors

Rae wants to be a park ranger.

What do they do?

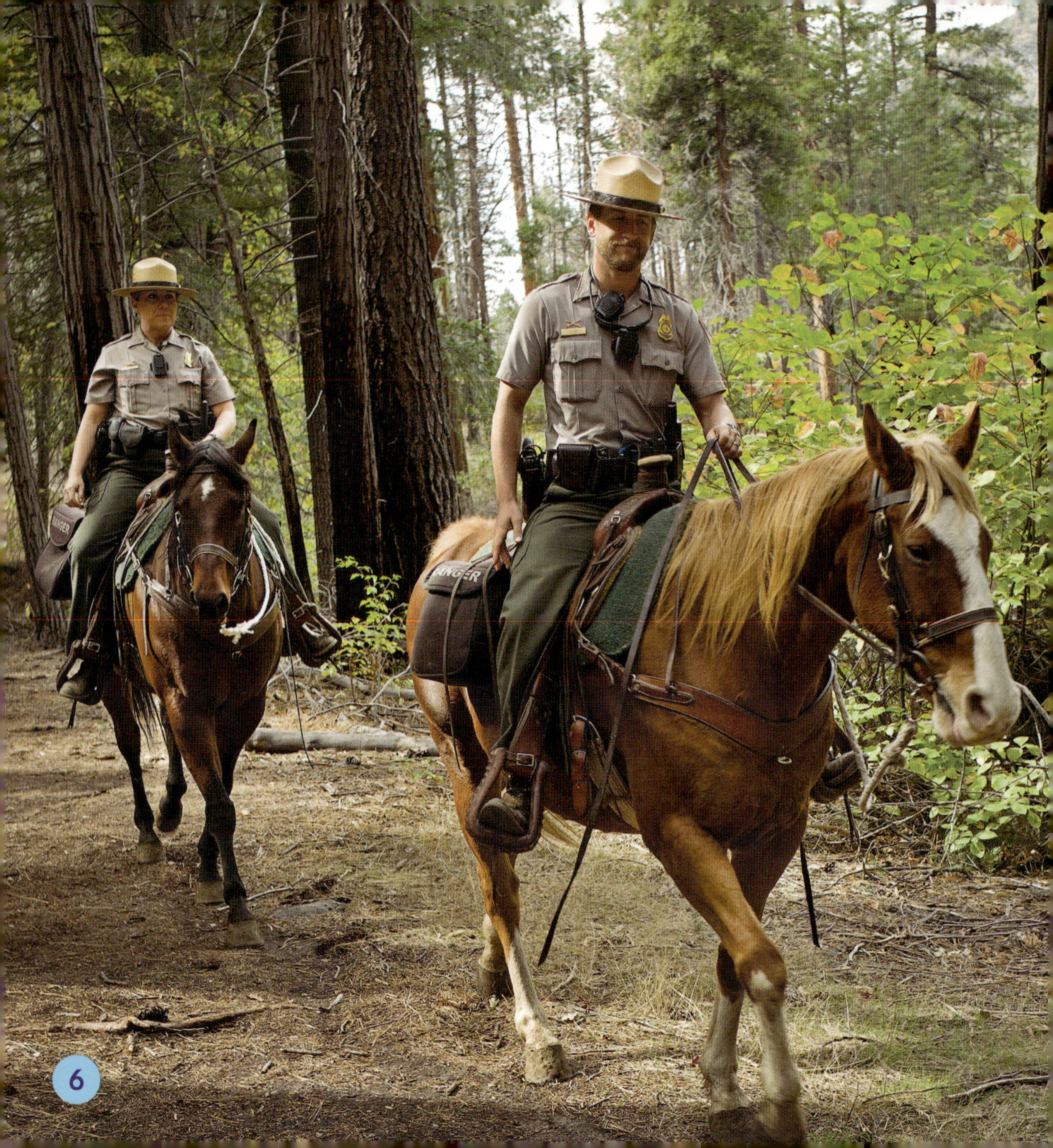

They protect our parks.

The plants, animals, and people in them, too!

Al is a ranger.

How do we know?

He wears a uniform.

He knows a lot about the park.

uniform

9

Jason is a ranger.

He shows us to our campsite.

Thanks, Jason!

These hikers need directions.

Cal knows the park well.

He has a map, too.

Cal shows them where to go.

map

14

Our class visits the park.

We hike.

We learn how to read the signs.

17

We learn about wildlife.

We get to be junior rangers! Fun!

20

Park rangers do good work!

At the Visitor Center

park ranger
A park ranger works at the park's visitor center. He or she is there to answer your questions about the park.

map
The visitor center has maps you can use to help you hike, camp, and explore the park.

Picture Glossary

directions
Instructions for finding a place.

protect
To guard or keep something safe from harm or damage.

uniform
A special set of clothes worn by members of a certain organization or group.

wildlife
Wild animals living in their natural habitat.

Index

animals 7
campsite 10
directions 12
hike 16
hikers 12
junior rangers 19
map 12
parks 7, 8, 12, 15
plants 7
protect 7
signs 16
uniform 8

To Learn More

Finding more information is as easy as 1, 2, 3.

❶ Go to www.factsurfer.com
❷ Enter "parkrangers" into the search box.
❸ Choose your book to see a list of websites.